Richard the Party Pig

By Kathryn and
Byron Jackson

A GOLDEN BOOK • NEW YORK

Copyright © 1954 and copyright renewed 1982 by Penguin Random House LLC
All rights reserved. Published in the United States by Golden Books, an imprint of
Random House Children's Books, a division of Penguin Random House LLC,
1745 Broadway, New York, NY 10019. Originally published in the United States
and in slightly different form by Simon and Schuster, Inc., and Artists and Writers
Guild, Inc., New York, in 1954. Golden Books, A Golden Book, A Little Golden Book,
the G colophon, and the distinctive gold spine are registered trademarks and
A Little Golden Book Classic is a trademark of Penguin Random House LLC.
rhcbooks.com
Educators and librarians, for a variety of teaching tools,
visit us at RHTeachersLibrarians.com
Library of Congress Control Number: 2018946518
ISBN 978-1-9848-4987-8 (trade) —
ISBN 978-1-9848-4988-5 (ebook)
Printed in the United States of America
10 9 8 7 6 5 4 3 2 1

One day it was Little Pig's birthday.
He had new red overalls that fit just right,
a new blue rocking chair that rocked high
and low, and a new white handkerchief, in
case he sneezed.

And that wasn't all.

The pantry in Little Pig's house was jammed and crammed with everything for a dandy birthday party— everything but a birthday cake.

But at that very moment, his mother was on her way to market to get some flour so she could bake a cake for him.

"My cake will be big and high," Little Pig said dreamily to himself. "With thick pink icing and thin pink candles and bright, shiny lights on top of every single one!"

Just then, he heard someone squeak, "I'm hungry!"

There in the yard was such a hungry-looking little mouse that Little Pig ran into the pantry and brought out the party cheese and all the party candy.

"There, Mouse!" he said. "How's that?"

"Excellent!" laughed the mouse. He piled them into his wheelbarrow and trudged off, looking so happy and friendly that Little Pig called after him, "Come to my birthday party! Six o'clock sharp! Games and prizes!"

"I'll be there!" called the mouse.

No sooner had the mouse left than Little Pig heard a sad mewing sound. He parted the bushes and found a small striped kitten.

"I'm hungry, too," she sobbed. "Terribly hungry!"

Little Pig ran into the pantry again. This time he brought out the tuna fish salad, the pitcher of milk, and the cream. The kitten gobbled it all up, thanked Little Pig, and went off with her little sides bulging.

"Come back for my birthday party," he called after her. "Six o'clock sharp, and there'll be games and prizes!"

And then, before Little Pig had time to think that there would be no cheese or candy or fish or cream for his party, a ragged puppy trotted up, crying for some meat. A stickly porcupine bumbled up, moaning because his mother had no sugar for her baking.

A skinny calf stumbled up, crying for some apples.
A sad woolly lamb wandered up, bleating for some
nice green spinach. And then a shabby little boy
walked slowly up the path, wishing for some bread
with butter and jelly.

Little Pig felt awfully sorry for all those thin,
hungry folks!

He ran in and out of the pantry, giving them all of his birthday goodies. He asked every single one to come back for his birthday party, too.

"We wouldn't miss your party, with games and prizes, for anything!" they called.

And when they left, smiling and skipping and hugging their packages, there was nothing left in the pantry except a dozen eggs.

But Little Pig never even noticed that. He just thought, "Goodness! I have no prizes!" And he hurried into the dining room to make some.

He made them out of paper, paste, crayons, and pins. Then he set the table.

"Happy birthday to me," he hummed, "happy birthday to us, happy birthday to my party—I love all this fuss!"

Just as he was finishing his song, Little Pig heard a timid knock on the door.

There was the sorriest-looking hen Little Pig had ever seen.

"Deary, deary me," she cried. "I'm going to be done away with because I can't lay eggs!"

So Little Pig slipped into the pantry, took out the eggs, and gave them to the hen, who went off cackling as proudly as if she had laid them herself. And while he was making a prize for her, his mother came home.

Into the kitchen she went, and out she ran again.

"Little Pig!" she cried. "Every last bit of your birthday dinner is gone!"

"Yes, Mother," said Little Pig. "So many hungry folks came to see me today that I gave everything away—I guess."

"Oh, Little Pig!" his mother said. "It's fine to be generous, but we can't have a party when there's nothing in the house to eat!"

"N-no party?" whispered Little Pig in a shaky voice. "Couldn't we just have birthday cake?"

But his mother shook her head. "There won't even be a cake," she said, "because I can't make a cake with nothing but flour."

Poor Little Pig!

He looked at the prizes he had made. He looked at the table he had set. He thought about all the guests he'd invited for six o'clock sharp, and he sat down and cried as if his little heart would break.

While he was crying, the clock began to strike. It struck one, and two, and three, and four, and five, and six—and just as it struck six, there were all sorts of knocks on the door, and all kinds of voices began to sing, "Happy birthday, Little Pig!"

Then the door flew open, and all his friends came marching in.

In came the mouse, his little wheelbarrow piled high with lollipops and peppermint sticks, and a rich cheese balanced on his head.

Next came the kitten with a tray of broiled fish, and the puppy with a roast turkey. The porcupine had a basket of hot rolls his mother had baked and a pitcher of milk from the calf's mama.

The hen carried a little pie she had baked herself, with the words "Little Pig" cut into the crispy crust.

The lamb brought a big bowl of buttery mushrooms, and the calf a bigger one of cinnamon applesauce.

Last of all came the boy. He had an enormous cake with thick pink icing and thin pink candles! Little Pig was so surprised and happy that he couldn't say a word.

He kissed his mother and hugged his friends. He smiled all over his happy little face, and he wiped the tears off his new red overalls.

And then the party began.

It was a tremendous party!

There has never been one like it before or since. Everyone ate, and joked, and laughed, and shook hands over and over again.

When at last the feast had ended, the wonderful
games began. And when Little Pig gave out the prizes,
it just so happened that in one game or another,
everyone at the party had won a first prize!